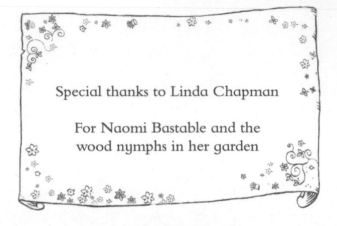

Special thanks to Linda Chapman

For Naomi Bastable and the
wood nymphs in her garden

ORCHARD BOOKS

First published in Great Britain in 2014 by Orchard Books
This edition published in 2017 by The Watts Publishing Group

7 9 10 8

© 2014 Hothouse Fiction Limited
Illustrations © Orchard Books 2014

A CIP catalogue record for this book is available from the British Library.

ISBN 978 1 40832 916 0

Printed in Great Britain by Clays Ltd, St Ives plc

MIX
Paper from
responsible sources
FSC® C104740

The paper and board used in this book are made from wood from responsible sources

Orchard Books
An imprint of Hachette Children's Group
Part of The Watts Publishing Group Limited
Carmelite House, 50 Victoria Embankment, London EC4Y 0DZ

An Hachette UK Company
www.hatchette.co.uk
www.hachettechildrens.co.uk

Series created by Hothouse Fiction
www.hothousefiction.com

Pixie Princess

ROSIE BANKS

This is the
Secret Kingdom

The Heart Tree

Book One

Contents

Ready For Adventure!   11

The Heart Tree   25

Coming Home   37

Under Attack!   49

A New Pixie Princess   69

Trixi Fights Back   85

Ready For Adventure!

Boing! Boing! Ellie Macdonald, Summer Hammond and Jasmine Smith jumped up and down on the trampoline in Jasmine's back garden. The sun was shining brightly in the clear blue sky.

"This is fun!" cried Ellie, her red curls bouncing around.

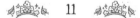

"Watch me!" Jasmine tried to turn a somersault but she ended up in a heap at their feet. "Whoops!"

Giggling, Ellie and Summer flopped down beside her. "It's so warm!" said Summer pushing back her blonde plaits and fanning her face.

Jasmine rolled on to her back. "I feel like I'm going to melt."

Ellie grinned as she thought of a joke. "What do you call a dog on a day like this?"

"What?" the others said.

"A hot dog!" Ellie giggled as Jasmine and Summer both groaned. Ellie had a thought and glanced around to check that Jasmine's mum wasn't near the trampoline. "I wonder if it's this warm in the Secret Kingdom at the moment," she said in a low voice.

"Oh, I wish we could go there to find out!" said Summer longingly.

Jasmine nodded. "I really feel like going on a Secret Kingdom adventure today."

"I feel like going on one *every* day!" Ellie grinned.

The three girls had a very special secret – they were the only people that knew

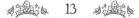

about a magical world called the Secret Kingdom! Ellie smiled as she imagined its lush meadows, rolling hills, tall mountains and sparkling seas. They had made so many friends there – pixies, unicorns, mermaids and elves – as well as the lovely King Merry who ruled the land, and his royal pixie Trixibelle who looked after him. "Do you remember when Trixi made us small and we went to Glitter Beach and helped all the fairies there?" she said.

"Oh, yes," breathed Summer. "It was amazing!"

Ellie sat up. "Why don't we go and check the Magic Box now and see if Trixi's sent us a message? Where is it, Jasmine?"

The girls always took it in turns to look

after the Magic Box. At the moment, Jasmine was taking care of it. "It's in my old ballet bag in my wardrobe," Jasmine said. "Come on, we can get a cool drink at the same time."

They jumped off the trampoline and ran into the house. Then they poured out some chilled apple juice into glasses and went up to Jasmine's bedroom. Her walls were painted a bright pink, she had pretty pink netting over her bed and a stripy pink-and-white duvet cover. On her walls she had stuck up posters of pop stars and actresses and dancers.

"Oh, wouldn't it be brilliant if there was a message for us from Trixi or King Merry?" Jasmine said as she finished her apple juice. Putting the glass down, she opened the wardrobe.

Sparkling light shone out, even brighter than the sunshine outside. Summer gasped and Ellie nearly spilled her drink in delight! At the bottom of the wardrobe the Magic Box was sparkling inside Jasmine's ballet bag. It could only mean one thing...

"There's a new message for us!" cried Jasmine.

Summer ran to shut the bedroom door while Jasmine picked up the bag and pulled out the wooden box. Its sides were carved and studded with gems and there was a mirror set into its curved lid. Jasmine placed it gently on the floor

and they all crouched down. Words were already swirling across the surface of the mirror.

Jasmine read them out, her heart beating fast:

"A glittering school with walls of white,
Heart Tree with leaves that shine so bright,
Pixies playing, leaves in the sky –
Guess the riddle, it's time to fly!"

As she spoke the last word the box opened by itself and a map of the Secret Kingdom floated up, unfolding in front of them. All the pictures on it magically moved, showing what was happening in the kingdom as if they were looking at it through a window. The girls grinned as they saw the flags waving from the pink turrets of King Merry's Enchanted Palace, mermaids splashing in the aquamarine sea and bubblebees buzzing near Bubble Volcano.

Summer sighed with delight as she looked at the familiar crescent-shaped island. "There's only one place the riddle could mean. It's got to be the Leafy Lands, where the Pixie Flying School is." She pointed to a forest where tiny pixies were swooping around on leaves. A small white building with a golden roof was nestled between the trees. It had four sides surrounding an open grassy area in the middle, where tiny pixies learnt to fly their leaves.

"You're right," agreed Ellie. "The riddle says it's a school and a place where pixies play..."

"But I wonder what the Heart Tree is?" Jasmine added.

Summer grinned. "Hopefully we'll soon find out!" She touched two of the gems on the box and the others did the same.

"Leafy Lands!" they all chorused.

There was a green flash and out of the Magic Box shot a little pixie riding on a leaf. She was wearing a green dress and had a chain of wild flowers on her golden hair.

"Hello, girls!" she cried, flying the leaf over to kiss each of them on the nose, balancing on the leaf as if it was a surfboard.

"Trixi!" cried the girls.

"I'm glad you got my message," said Trixi as the map folded itself back into the box and the lid shut with a snap.

"Is something wrong in the Secret Kingdom?" Ellie asked. They normally got messages when there was a problem that King Merry needed their help solving. Usually it was because his horrible sister, Queen Malice, had thought up a wicked plan to try and become the ruler of the Secret Kingdom. Luckily, the girls had always managed to stop her!

"Oh, no. Nothing's wrong this time," said Trixi.

"Phew!" said Summer in relief.

"So why did you send us a message?" Jasmine asked curiously.

Trixi beamed. "Because it's a special time in the Leafy Lands. Tomorrow is Graduation Day – that's the day that all the pixies who are ready to leave the Pixie Flying School get their own grown-up leaves. I thought you might like to come along and help us get ready. It'll be lots of fun. Then tomorrow you could come to the ceremony. My little cousin, Petal, is graduating and she's very excited." Trixi gave them a hopeful look. "Would you like to come?"

"Oh, yes please!" the girls cried.

"Will you make us pixie-sized again like you did last time we went to the flying school?" Summer asked eagerly.

Trixi nodded. "You'll have to be small

to be able to explore the Heart Tree properly."

"What is the Heart Tree?" Ellie asked.

Trixi's eyes sparkled in excitement. "That's where I live – it's my home!"

The Heart Tree

Jasmine, Summer and Ellie grinned at each other – they couldn't wait to see Trixi's home! Trixi tapped the green pixie ring on her finger and called out a spell.

*"Magic ring, take my friends three
As pixies small, to the Heart Tree!"*

A sparkling cloud of light surrounded the girls, whisking them off their feet.

They spun round and round, feeling
themselves growing smaller and smaller
until they finally landed with a bump on
something soft and bouncy – a bit like
Jasmine's trampoline.

Summer opened her eyes and saw she
was sitting on a wide green leaf that was
floating in the air! She looked around
for her friends and saw that Jasmine
and Ellie were also on leaves beside
her. Beautiful tiaras had appeared on
their heads. Summer smiled and lifted
one hand to touch it.

Their tiaras appeared whenever they
came to the Secret Kingdom and
showed everyone that the girls were Very
Important Friends of King Merry.

"We're flying!"
cried Jasmine,
starting to zoom
around on her leaf.

On one of their
other adventures
they'd flown on
pixie leaves.
The leaves they
were on now
were just like the ones
that young pixies used when
they were learning to fly. They
were broad and flat with turned-up
edges like little walls. As Trixi swooped

up and down, Jasmine stood up and tried to remember what to do to make the leaf go.

Lean to the left to make it go left, she thought, grinning with excitement as her leaf sped off. "Wheeeeeee!" she yelled.

Summer sat on her leaf and looked around. They were so small now that the flowers seemed as tall as trees and the trees as tall as mountains! She saw a blue butterfly flutter up to a flower. It was as big as the leaf she was sitting on!

She flew closer to get a better look. Summer loved all animals and it was amazing to see the beautiful details of the butterfly's wings. Then she spotted a dragonfly and zoomed after it eagerly.

Unlike Summer, Ellie stuck close to Trixi. Although she had learnt to fly a leaf last time they came to the Leafy Lands, she didn't like heights and she was glad of the turned up edges of the leaf – they made her feel much safer.

"This way!" Trixi called, beckoning Summer and Jasmine. "Follow me to the Heart Tree!"

Summer and Jasmine flew over and the four of them set off through the forest. They swooped round bushes and flowers until Trixi finally came to a stop. She pointed ahead. "There!" she said proudly.

The girls caught their breath. A huge tree towered up in front of them. It looked a bit like an oak tree, but its leaves were shaped like gorgeous green hearts! A slight breeze rustled them and they chimed like tiny bells. But it wasn't just the beautiful leaves that made the girls gasp. The wide branches of the tree were dotted

with houses, all with
thatched roofs and
round windows.
It was like a little
village in a tree!
Slatted wooden
walkways lit by
glowing balls of
light joined
one branch
to another and
pixies were skipping
along the walkways,
standing in the doors
of the houses, hanging
out brightly coloured
washing and flying
through the branches
on their leaves.

"So this is the Heart Tree?" breathed Summer. She couldn't tear her eyes away from the amazing tree. She gazed from the huge tangled roots up to the heart-shaped leaves. There was even a heart-shaped knot hole in the smooth bark of the trunk, with pixies flying their leaves in and out of it. She didn't think she'd ever seen a tree so beautiful.

"Yes." Trixi's eyes glowed. "This is where I live."

"But I thought you lived at Enchanted Palace with King Merry," Jasmine said in surprise.

"I do live there some of the time, but this is where I grew up," said Trixi. "Follow me! My mum should be home!"

"Your mum?" Ellie echoed, flying after her. They'd met Trixi's Aunt Maybelle before when they'd been trying to stop Queen Malice turning King Merry into a stink toad, but they hadn't met the rest of Trixi's family. Ellie couldn't wait to see her!

"Yes! This way!" Trixi laughed. They flew up through the branches. The pixies they passed spotted the girls' tiaras and waved and called out greetings. Summer was looking forward to stopping to explore the tree properly. The houses looked so sweet and the pixies were all so friendly!

Trixi landed her leaf on a wide branch

near the top of the tree. "Here we are," she said. In front of her was a little house with sky-blue shutters and round windows. The front door was also painted blue and had a brass knocker in the shape of an acorn. The girls followed

Trixi as she brought her leaf down to land on the branch outside the house.

"Mum!" Trixi called. "I'm home!"

Coming Home

The door opened and a slim pixie with blonde shoulder-length hair came running out. She looked just like an older version of Trixi! "Trixibelle!" she cried. Trixi and the girls jumped off their leaves and Trixi hugged her mum. "I'm so glad you could come home for graduation day!" her mum said.

"I wouldn't miss it for the whole kingdom!" declared Trixi. "And Mum, I brought King Merry's special friends to meet you. This is Summer, Ellie and Jasmine."

Her mum's hands flew to her face in delight. "Oh, how wonderful!" she said. "Welcome to the Heart Tree, girls. I'm Bluebell." She came forward and gave them each a hug. "I can't believe I'm meeting you at last. Trixi's told me all about the adventures you've had together. It sounds like you've saved her from dreadful trouble lots of times."

"And she's saved us, too," said Ellie loyally. "We couldn't have stopped Queen Malice without her. She's so brave."

"And does such brilliant magic," Jasmine agreed.

"She's wonderful!" said Summer.
Trixi went as pink as a rose and
Bluebell looked proud enough to burst!

"I always knew she would grow up to be
a royal pixie," she confessed to the girls.
"Only the bravest and cleverest pixies are
chosen to be a royal pixie. It's a great
honour. But I knew from the start that
Trixi would be one. She's always loved

having adventures. I remember the time she heard a baby unicorn had got lost and she set off to find him all by herself. She was only five years old!" She shook her head affectionately at her daughter.

Trixi looked embarrassed. "Mum! Stop it!" she giggled. She glanced looked at the girls. "Why don't you come inside?"

"Oh, yes please!" said Summer excitedly. The house was so cute she couldn't wait to see inside! They followed Trixi into the front room. The floors were made of polished wood with brightly coloured rugs covering them, and there were lots of photos of Trixi lined up over a little fireplace. Bluebell showed them through to a cosy kitchen with herbs and pots and pans hanging from the ceiling. She handed round a plate of freshly-baked honey cookies and little acorn cups filled with a sweet icy drink. "It's nectar lemonade," she said.

"It's delicious!" said Ellie as the drink fizzed and sparkled on her tongue. Normal lemonade would never taste as nice again!

"Can we see your bedroom, Trixi?"

asked Jasmine.

"Of course!" Trixi said, leading them through the house. Her bedroom was small and cosy with a patchwork bedspread on the bed. The walls were decorated with maps of the Secret Kingdom. Little silver hearts glowed in different places on the maps. "What are they?" asked Summer curiously.

Trixi smiled. "I like to mark the places

I've been." She pointed to some. "We've been to lots of these together – Bubble Volcano, Jewel Cavern—"

"Dolphin Bay!" said Ellie pointing to a pretty cove.

"And Magic Mountain," said Jasmine, looking at an icy mountain with pixies skiing down it.

"You've been all over the kingdom!" said Summer. There were glowing hearts everywhere on the map!

"I'm really lucky," said Trixi. "Being a royal pixie is the perfect job for me!"

Just then the door flew open and another pixie came running in. "Trixi! You're back!" The little pixie was a bit younger than Trixi and was wearing a blue floaty dress. She ran into the room and hugged Trixi.

"This is my cousin, Petal," Trixi explained. "Petal, these are King Merry's special friends – Ellie, Summer and Jasmine."

Petal squealed. "Really?" She looked at the girls in awe. "Oh, this is so amazing! Just wait till I tell Daisy, Honeysuckle and Foxglove that I've met you. Everyone at school talks about the adventures you've had. You're so brave to fight Queen Malice. Have you come for Graduation Day?"

Summer nodded. "Trixi said you're graduating tomorrow."

Petal nodded, her blue eyes shining. "I can't wait. At the ceremony I'll get to find out what sort of pixie I'll be."

The girls exchanged puzzled looks. "What do you mean?" asked Jasmine.

"On Graduation Day, each pixie who is graduating approaches the Heart Tree," Trixi explained. "They ask the tree for a leaf and the tree chooses them one. Some get leaves that fly high, others that fly fast, others that are safe and slow. Each pixie gets a grown-up leaf that is perfect for them and when they get it they find out what sort of job they'll do."

"Like whether they'll be a waterfall pixie or a mountain pixie or a forest pixie or a seashore pixie – or even a

royal pixie, like Trixi!" added Petal.
"There are lots of different pixie jobs.
We have to take care of the whole of the
Secret Kingdom. I like flying high so I
really want to be a mountain pixie." She
spun round, making her skirt twirl out
around her.

"The ceremony's very exciting," said
Trixi to the girls. "King Merry always
comes along to be in charge of it."

"It's going to be the most perfect day
ever!" declared Petal.

But as she spoke there was a loud noise
overhead and a crash shook the branches
of the tree so hard that the girls and
pixies stumbled and fell over. "What's
happening?" asked Petal, scrambling to
her feet in alarm.

"I'm not sure," said Trixi.

"Trixi! Come quick!" Bluebell shouted.

They all raced out of the bedroom. There was another deafening bang and the tree shook violently again. They had to cling on to the furniture to stay on their feet. Bluebell was standing by the open front door.

"What's going on, Mum?" Trixi shouted.

Bluebell gasped, her face pale. "The Heart Tree is under attack!"

Under Attack!

"Come on!" said Jasmine to the others. They charged out of the house and leaped onto their leaves. Other pixies were running along the branches, and everyone was shouting and yelling.

Ellie noticed something. "Look at Trixi's ring!"

Magical light was spilling out of it.

"Everyone's ring is glowing!" Summer realised. "Trixi! Look!"

"The pixie magic in our rings is uniting to protect the tree," gasped Trixi. "If the tree is ever under attack then all the rings start working to put a magic barrier around it."

"But who would attack the Heart Tree?" said Petal.

"I can think of one person," Jasmine said grimly.

BANG!

The pixies around them screamed as the tree's branches creaked and groaned.

A cackling laugh filled the air, growing louder and louder.

The girls stared at each other. They knew that laugh.

"It's Queen Malice," whispered Summer.

The girls ran to the end of the branch as a tall bony figure stepped into the

clearing and faced the Heart Tree.
Summer was right – it *was* Queen
Malice! Wild
black hair
surrounded
her pale face
and her eyes
glinted icily. She
held a black staff
in one hand and
looked absolutely
enormous now
the girls were
pixie-sized.

  Jasmine
gasped as
she saw
the huge,
horrid queen.

Queen Malice's pointed nose alone was almost as big as she was, and her face blocked out the sun. But Jasmine was too angry to feel scared. "Stop it!" she shouted to the queen. "Stop attacking the tree!"

Queen Malice peered closer. Her eyebrows arched as she spotted Jasmine, Summer and Ellie. "Well, well, well," she said, her voice sounding horribly loud.

"It's you three pesky human girls again. Trying to interfere, no doubt."

"You're the one who's interfering!" said Jasmine bravely. "Leave us alone!"

"Yes, go away!" cried Ellie.

"Whatever you're trying to do, it won't work!" Summer shouted.

"Oh really," sneered the horrid queen.

Trixi came forward. "The girls are right. Our pixie magic will protect the Heart Tree."

Queen Malice's eyes narrowed and she reached out towards the heart-shaped knot at the centre of the tree. "We'll see about that... *Ow!*" she shrieked as a bright green light flashed across her fingers. She pulled her hand back, shaking it. "That hurt!" she said, looking outraged.

A few of the pixies giggled nervously.

"I told you, our pixie magic protects this tree!" cried Trixi. "Now, go away!"

"No!" snarled Queen Malice, raising her thunderbolt staff.

CRASH! The tree shook as another thunderbolt slammed into its branches. The pixies yelled and hung on to one another, and the heart-shaped leaves chimed together loudly.

"You can't beat me!" Queen Malice crowed. "I can keep sending thunderbolts all day. No silly pixie magic can withstand that for long."

Bluebell flew her leaf forward. "Please don't do this, Queen Malice. What have the pixies ever done to you?"

Queen Malice drew herself up to her full height. "I will stop..." She paused to give a cruel smile. Ellie, Jasmine and Summer looked at each other anxiously. "If you give me the Pixie Princess's crown!" the wicked queen snapped.

"No!" shouted Trixi.

All the other pixies seemed as shocked as Trixi. They were talking quickly in low voices, frowning and shaking their heads.

What's going on? Jasmine thought. She had never heard of a pixie princess or her crown!

Queen Malice raised her staff again.

"Quick, everyone!" cried Trixi. "Fly to the Heart Hall!"

Everyone flew their leaves up into
the air and Jasmine, Summer and Ellie
followed. The pixies whizzed off, heading
for the heart-shaped knot hole in the
centre of the tree trunk. Queen Malice
swatted at them like flies but the pixies
darted and dodged around her flapping
hands. One by one they zoomed towards
the hole and swooped inside.

Jasmine, Summer and Ellie flew
in through the knot hole and found
themselves inside the tree in an enormous
hall. Its walls were made of polished
wood and they were carved with
beautiful old-fashioned writing. The floor
was covered in an enormous circular
rug that had pictures of pretty pixies
woven into its soft material, and garlands
of flowers decorated the high domed
ceiling. In one corner of the room was
a glittering crystal pedestal and on top
of the pedestal was a glass box with a
twinkling pink crown inside.

The girls landed their leaves on the
floor by the pedestal and jumped off.
Everyone was talking anxiously and
the room was getting noisy with the
concerned chatter. Some of the pixies

were crying and others were comforting them.

Summer couldn't bear to watch the miserable pixies. She turned away and

walked over to the glass box on the pedestal. *They had to help!* The crown was a circle of pink pearls, covered with gorgeous flowers and tiny butterflies. Jasmine and Ellie joined her and the three friends stared at the crown in wonder.

"Isn't it beautiful?" said Ellie above the din.

"It certainly is," a soft voice said. The girls swung round and saw an older pixie coming over to them. She was wearing a long, elegant green dress, her grey hair was in a neat bun on top of her head and she wore tiny silver glasses.

"Aunt Maybelle!" cried Summer.

"Hello, girls," said Aunt Maybelle.

She tapped her ring and the girls felt the noise of the rest of the room fade away slightly, as if they and Aunt Maybelle were in a separate magic bubble, far away from the chatter all around them.

"It's lovely to see you, even in these terrible circumstances." As she spoke the tree shook again with the force of another thunderbolt.

"Is this the crown Queen Malice wants?" asked Jasmine.

Aunt Maybelle nodded. "Yes, this is the pixie princess's crown. It doubles the power of whoever wears it, making the princess the most powerful pixie in the land."

"We never even knew the pixies had a princess," said Summer. "Who is she?"

Aunt Maybelle sighed. "There *is* no pixie princess. Many moons ago, before King Merry ruled the Secret Kingdom, the land was ruled by King Moody. He made everyone very unhappy. The pixies kept away from him, living in the

Heart Tree and obeying their own pixie princess. But when King Merry became king. there was no need for the pixies to have their own leader anymore. When the old princess reached the end of her life and faded away into sparkling light, the Heart Tree sent a message telling the pixies to put the crown away in this glass case. The Heart Tree said that it would stay locked away until a new pixie princess was needed."

"Only now Queen Malice has decided she wants it," said Ellie as the tree shook again.

"Yes," said Aunt Maybelle. "And I fear she will not stop attacking the tree until she gets it."

"But it won't even fit her!" Ellie said indignantly.

"The crown would magically grow to her size," Aunt Maybelle said sadly. "And if she owns it — her power will be doubled!"

"We won't let that happen!" Jasmine said fiercely. Summer and Ellie nodded.

Just then Trixi came running over. "Aunt Maybelle!" she said anxiously. "How long can our pixie magic defend the tree?"

"Not for much longer." Aunt Maybelle held out her hand. The light in her pixie ring was flickering. "Look, our power is already getting weaker. As the power gets used up, the light in our rings will fade," Aunt Maybelle explained, her voice trembling. "When they go dark, all our hope is gone..."

Summer gasped and Trixi buried her face in her hands with a sob.

"If only there was a pixie princess, she could wear the crown and use her power to stop Queen Malice," said Jasmine thoughtfully.

"Yes!" cried Ellie. "Can't you choose a new princess?"

"I'm afraid not," sighed Aunt Maybelle. "The Heart Tree alone can decide when a new princess should be chosen. Until that happens the glass case will stay locked with the crown inside."

"Oh, please, Heart Tree! Please choose a princess!" Summer begged looking round. She touched the nearby wall. "The pixies really need your help."

"Summer! Look!" Ellie exclaimed. Light was sparking out from under Summer's fingers.

Summer removed her hand with a gasp.

Some of the words carved into the walls were glowing brightly.

"The Heart Tree is sending us a message!" cried Aunt Maybelle.

A New Pixie Princess

Trixi jumped on her leaf and flew into the air. "Quiet, everyone!" she shouted, sending a green ball of light flying above their heads. "Please be quiet!" The ball of light exploded into a thousand green sparks. It caught everyone's attention and for a moment they all stopped talking.

"The Heart Tree is sending us a message," cried Trixi, making everyone gasp in excitement.

"It looks like part of a riddle," said Aunt Maybelle from beside the glowing writing. She held up her hand and when there was silence she read the words out:

"The new pixie princess is near to royal…"

Aunt Maybelle looked round, her eyes shining. "This is wonderful! I think the

Heart Tree has chosen a new princess!"

"Look!" said Jasmine suddenly. "There are more words lit up over there too!" She ran to the opposite wall and read out four glowing words: *"She's clever and kind..."*

Ellie spotted some other words and read them out: *"Brave and loyal!"*

The pixies started running round too, each calling out the words they found.

"She's been...

"...far further..."

"...than this tree."

"Who'll wear..."

"...the crown?"

"You'll soon see!" cried Summer as she read the last few words.

Aunt Maybelle repeated the whole thing.

"*The new Pixie Princess is near to royal,*
   She's clever and kind, brave and loyal.
   She's been far further than this tree.
   Who'll wear the crown? You'll soon see!"

Suddenly the glass casket cracked into tiny pieces that vanished as they fell to the floor. The crown floated out of the case and hovered at head height.

"So, which pixie is going to be the princess?" said Summer excitedly.

"Oh, I hope it's me!" cried Petal.

"The riddle gives us some clues," said Jasmine thoughtfully. "It's someone who's

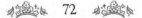

travelled further than the tree."

Petal looked disappointed. "Oh, I haven't."

"What does that bit mean about the princess being near to royal?" Ellie puzzled. "Is anyone here related to royalty?"

The pixies all shook their heads.

"Okay, well let's ignore that particular clue for now. Who *has* travelled far from the tree?" said Jasmine.

At least half the pixies put up their hands.

Outside there was another crash and the light in the pixies' rings faded even more. "There's no time to waste solving the riddle," Aunt Maybelle said quickly. "I think everyone who has travelled far should try on the crown. I have a feeling the crown will show us who the princess should be."

"You start, Aunt Maybelle," said Trixi. "You're the cleverest, kindest, bravest and most loyal pixie I know."

Aunt Maybelle went and stood beneath

the crown, but nothing happened. The
other pixies formed a line. There was no
pushing or shoving, everyone just looked
very anxious.

Time's running out, Summer thought
desperately. If they didn't find the princess
fast then Queen Malice would break
down the tree's defences and take the
crown by force. One by one the pixies
took it in turns to stand under the crown,
but it still stayed hovering there.

As Bluebell stepped towards the crown, there was a shout from the entrance to the knot hole. "Oh, no!" Trixi yelled. "The Storm Sprites are here!"

Summer, Jasmine and Ellie ran to the knot hole and looked out to see four creatures with grey skin and bat-like wings flapping around the tree. In the middle of them was Queen Malice – and she was raising her staff for another strike!

"She's about to throw another thunderbolt!" yelled Jasmine. "And she's aiming straight for us. Hold on everyone!"

BANG! A thunderbolt hit the tree trunk. Trixi and the girls were thrown backwards with the blast. They scrambled to their feet and saw that a jagged

splintered hole had appeared in the
trunk. The pixies' protection magic
was disappearing!

"Fetch me that crown!" they heard
Queen Malice shriek.

An eye appeared at the knot hole
and then a huge arm shot into the hall.
The pixies screamed and leaped back as

the spindly fingers swept around, trying to grab the crown. Trixi ran over and grabbed the crown, pulling it out of the sprite's reach just in time. She jumped back, holding the crown close. Suddenly, it started to shine and glitter. The pixies all gasped.

"What's happening?" stammered Trixi, looking at it in amazement.

The crown rose into the air and Trixi let it go. The pixies all fell silent as it hovered above Trixi's head and

then floated down again to land gently
on her golden hair.

Before Trixi could say anything there
was a screech from outside. The Storm
Sprite was peering in again, his eye
pressed to the bark. "I'm going to have
that crown even if I have to take you
with it, you silly pixie!"

His eye disappeared and his arm came
sweeping in again.

Trixi reacted at lightning speed. She
tapped her ring and sent a circle of green

light hurtling towards the sprite's arm.
"Take that!" she cried.

The ball of light was so bright it hurt
the girls' eyes to look at it. It exploded
against the sprite's leathery skin in a
shower of sparks. With a furious howl he

pulled his arm back. "Ow! Ow! Ow!" he
screeched.

The girls and the pixies stared at Trixi.

She had stopped in the centre of the room and was staring at the her pixie ring as if she couldn't believe it. "What just happened?" she whispered.

"Trixi!" cried Ellie, looking at the crown. "Your magic powers have doubled because you're wearing the crown."

"You're the pixie princess!" Summer told her.

"I am?" Trixi said uncertainly, reaching up and touching the crown.

"Yes! Of course you are! It all makes sense now," said Jasmine. "The words in the riddle didn't mean the princess would actually *be* royal — it said she would be *near to royal* and you are because you're King Merry's royal pixie."

"You've certainly *travelled further than the tree*," added Ellie.

"And you're most definitely *brave, kind, clever and loyal*," finished Summer.

Trixi was speechless with astonishment.

"Oh, my Trixi!" cried Bluebell, running over and hugging her. She looked like she was about to burst with pride.

"Your Majesty," Aunt Maybelle curtseyed and all the other pixies sank down into deep bows.

"I'm really the pixie princess?" whispered Trixi, looking round.

"Yes," Aunt Maybelle said gently. "You are." She glanced at the entrance. "And now, my dear, you must use all your power to stop Queen Malice before she destroys our home forever!"

Trixi Fights Back

Trixi jumped on her leaf, flying straight out of the Heart Hall without looking back. The rest of the pixies, along with Jasmine, Summer and Ellie, grabbed their leaves and flew after her. Queen Malice was just raising her staff for another attack and the Storm Sprites were flapping around her on their leathery bat-like wings. One of them was holding his arm and looking very sulky.

"Come to surrender, have you?" Queen Malice cackled. "Ah! And there's my crown. Hand it over!"

"Never!" shouted Trixi fiercely. "It's not your crown – it's mine. I am the pixie princess and this tree and these pixies are under *my* protection!"

"Go, Trixi!" whooped Jasmine.

Queen Malice sneered. "You ridiculous little pixie. Even if your magic is doubled, you still won't be able to beat me!"

Trixi shook her head bravely. "I know, but I can still try. I'm the princess, and I'm not giving up without a fight!"

Trixi tapped her pixie ring, and something incredible happened – she started to grow!

Queen Malice gave a yelp of surprise as Trixi and her leaf grew bigger and bigger. Soon she was as tall as Queen Malice! She flew down so she was eye to eye with the nasty queen, and they both looked at each other in shock!

Queen Malice recovered first and gave a nasty sneer. "Ha! A party trick," she scoffed. She lifted her thunderbolt staff and pointed it at the Heart Tree. "Let's see what your precious tiara does when I turn your Heart Tree into matchsticks!"

"No!" Trixi interrupted, poking Queen Malice in the chest. "Leave my pixies and my home alone!" She tapped her ring and a glow sparkled from her ring and from her tiara.

"What are you doing?" Queen Malice stuttered.

"Casting a spell to make sure you never set foot near our Heart Tree again!" said Trixi bravely. She called out a spell:

"Queen Malice, look at me and fear.
You are never welcome here.
Step in these woods near our Heart Tree,
And you'll grow roots and never be free!"

Green light shot out from Trixi's ring
and tiara and surrounded the queen and
her horrible Storm Sprites. It spun them
round and round, tumbling them along
the ground and out of the woods like
giant pieces of tumbleweed.

"I'll get yooouu!"
Queen Malice's
shouts faded to
nothing as the
magic carried
her and the
sprites out to
the edge of the
woods.

Trixi turned to the
Heart Tree and looked
down at Jasmine, Summer,

Ellie and all the pixies. "I did it!" she gasped, looking astonished. "My magic finally worked against Queen Malice! If she comes here again she'll turn into a tree!" She tapped her ring and shrank back down to normal pixie size again. Then she flew back up to the branches of the Heart Tree.

"Hooray for Princess Trixibelle!" cried Petal as she landed. "Hip hip…"

"HOORAY!" they all cheered. Trixi looked delighted.

"You were so brave!" Summer said.

"Just amazing," said Ellie.

Trixi grinned. "I just thought about what you three would have done and tried to do the same."

They all smiled. "I'm so glad you're the Pixie Princess," said Jasmine.

"As princess, I declare we should all have a big party," announced Trixi. "Come on, everyone. Let's celebrate that Queen Malice has gone!

Another big cheer rang out and then everyone started hurrying about, fetching cakes, biscuits, fruit and big jugs of nectar lemonade and setting them out around the tree.

Summer, Jasmine and Ellie quickly volunteered to

help. They laid the tables, and were just about to help Petal put up some bunting when Summer noticed that someone was missing.

"Where's Trixi?" she said to Jasmine and Ellie.

They all looked round but they couldn't see their friend.

Summer spotted Aunt Maybelle looking around too. "Aunt Maybelle," she called. "Have you seen Trixi?"

Aunt Maybelle stopped. "No, I was just wondering where she had gone."

"Maybe she's gone back to her house," said Jasmine.

"Let's go and look," said Ellie.

Aunt Maybelle and the girls flew towards Bluebell's house. When they arrived, the door was open.

"Trixi?" called Ellie uncertainly.

There was a pause and then a small voice called from Trixi's bedroom. "I'm in here."

The girls and Aunt Maybelle looked at each other. Why was Trixi in her bedroom? They hurried along the corridor and into the bedroom. Trixi was sitting cross-legged on her bed. She was staring at the pictures on her wall sadly.

"Are you all right?" Summer asked, rushing over to put her arm around her.

Trixi swallowed. "Yes." She didn't sound all right though.

"What's the matter?" said Ellie.

Trixi wiped her eyes. "I was just thinking how much I'll miss being King Merry's royal pixie now I'm the princess. I love helping him."

"Oh, Trixi!" Aunt Maybelle said, taking her hands. "You won't have to stop being a royal pixie!"

Trixi stared at her. "I won't? But don't I have to stay here and protect the Heart Tree?"

"No, the pixie magic can do that!"

Aunt Maybelle smiled. "We will call you if we really need you, but otherwise we will manage just as we have for hundreds of years. One of the reasons I think the tree chose you to be the princess was *because* you travel around the kingdom and help King Merry. You mustn't stop doing that – as our princess it's even more important that you keep everyone in the kingdom safe. And most of all that means looking after King Merry, and helping Ellie, Summer and Jasmine stop Queen Malice."

The worry on Trixi's face melted away. "Oh, I'm so happy!" she cried, jumping up and she hugging them all. "Now, come on – we have a party to go to!"

The pixie party was wonderful fun.
The girls ate delicious treats and danced
around the trunk of the tree and then
had flying races with the other pixies.
As the sun set, the sky was streaked with
orange, gold and peach. One by one,
lights turned on in the pixie houses,
lighting the tree with a friendly glow.

At midnight, Aunt Maybelle told everyone it was time to go to bed. "Tomorrow is a very special day," she said. "We don't want to be too tired to enjoy the Graduation Ceremony!"

"Definitely not!" said Petal, turning a loop-the-loop on her leaf.

Trixi turned to Summer, Ellie and Jasmine. "I'll magic you home for now," she said, "but I'll send you a message tomorrow afternoon at two o'clock and then you can come and watch the Graduation Ceremony. In fact I make it a royal command! You *have* to be here!"

"Of course we'll be there, Your Highness!" Ellie giggled.

Trixi laughed too. "Until tomorrow then!"

She tapped her ring and the girls were

whisked away in a sparkling cloud. They landed back in Jasmine's bedroom.

"Wow! I can't believe Trixi is the Pixie Princess," said Ellie.

"I don't think she can quite believe it either," said Jasmine with a grin.

"Did you see Queen Malice's face when Trixi cast that spell on her," giggled Summer. "She looked furious!"

"And now she'll have to stay away from the Heart Tree forever," said Ellie.

"Unless she wants to grow roots and become a tree!" chuckled Jasmine. "I'd like to see that."

"Maybe we will," said Summer. "Who knows what will happen tomorrow?"

They exchanged excited looks. Tomorrow they would be back in the Secret Kingdom again. They simply couldn't wait!

Book
Two

Contents

Wobbling Along   105

Let the Ceremony Begin!   117

A Horrible Shock   129

Queen Malice's Plan   147

Cracking a Thunderbolt   161

Take That, Queen Malice!   173

Wobbling Along

"Look at me!" Molly called as she wobbled her bright pink bike down the woodland path. It was the next day, and Ellie's mum and dad had taken Ellie, Summer and Jasmine to Bramble Woods along with her little sister Molly for the afternoon. The girls had made sure to bring the Magic Box along with them. They didn't want to miss Trixi's message!

"Watch me!" Molly insisted.

"You're doing brilliantly, Molly," said Summer encouragingly. Molly had only just learned to ride her bike without stabilizers and she was still a bit shaky.

"Be careful, sweetie!" called Mrs Macdonald anxiously.

"I'm fine." Molly tried to look round at them all and grin but it made her sway from side to side.

"Watch out, Mol!" cried Ellie as Molly's front wheel hit a tree root. But it was too late! The bike wobbled and Molly tumbled off.

Ellie, Summer and Jasmine ran over, but luckily Molly wasn't hurt. She jumped to her feet and pulled her bike up. "I'm okay. I just need more practice. Soon I'll be as good at bike riding as all of you!"

She got on her bike and set off again, her red curls sticking out from under her bike helmet.

The girls ran after her along the footpath. "What's the time?" Summer whispered.

"Almost two o'clock," said Jasmine.

Ellie checked that her parents were safely out of earshot. "That means it's almost time for Trixi's message to appear in the Magic Box!"

"We need to be somewhere private when Trixi arrives," said Summer anxiously. "Somewhere your parents and Molly can't see us."

"I've got an idea," said Jasmine. She touched Summer on the arm. "You're it, Summer!" she shouted loudly so Ellie's parents could hear. "Bet you can't catch us. Come on, Ellie!"

She ran off the path into the trees.

Ellie raced after her. Summer grinned and raced after them. It was a brilliant plan to get away!

Jasmine stopped beside a large bush. Its branches were arching over, making a private cave behind the dark green leaves and bright pink flowers. "Let's all go in here," Jasmine urged. She held the branches to one side and she, Ellie and Summer ducked through them. They crouched down on the dusty ground and Jasmine pulled the beautiful box out of her bag.

She was just in time!

With a bright flash, words started swirling across the lid.

Summer felt a thrill of delight as she read the words out:

> "Dear friends, please come to
> our ceremony.
> There is no riddle, just say
> 'The Heart Tree!'"

The girls touched their hands to the box. "The Heart Tree!" they all whispered together.

There was a bright green flash and
Trixi appeared in the branches of the
bush. She was wearing
a beautiful purple
balldress with
silver swirls
on it. Around
her shoulders
was a gorgeous
little fur shrug,
attached by a
diamond clasp.
For once her
blonde hair
wasn't messily
peeking out from under a flower hat, but
swept up into a neat bun.

"You look so beautiful, Trixi!" gasped
Ellie.

Trixi beamed. "Thank you. As the new pixie princess I decided I'd better look smart for Graduation Day. It's such a special occasion. Oh, I can't wait to watch it and see Petal get her own grown-up leaf. I'm so glad you're all coming!"

"But Trixi, where's your crown?" asked Summer.

"It can't leave the Leafy Lands," Trixi explained. "It'll appear back on my head when we get there."

Jasmine looked at their jeans and t-shirts. "Will we be all right in these old clothes, Trixi?"

"Don't worry about that," Trixi grinned. "I'll use my magic to make sure you have some lovely dresses to wear. Hold hands!"

Exchanging excited looks, the girls grabbed one another's hands. They loved it when Trixi magicked them special clothes! Trixi tapped her ring. A cloud of sparkles surrounded them and swept them away, setting them down gently on a carpet of soft grass. They were pixie-sized again and were surrounded by tall, slender trees that seemed to go all the way up to the sky. Bluebirds were darting through the branches, singing merrily.

"There's the Heart Tree," said Summer,

spotting the beautiful tree a little way off. Its amazing heart-shaped leaves swayed in the breeze, tinkling gently.

"Look at our clothes!" exclaimed Jasmine doing a twirl. She was now wearing a pink dress, covered with ruffles and red flowers. Ellie was wearing a green dress with bows at the bottom, and yellow roses in her curly red hair and Summer had on a sunshine-yellow dress with a matching jewelled yellow bag.

"Do you like them?" said Trixi, flying around excitedly on her leaf.

"Oh yes!" they all cried.

"Should we go to the tree now?" Jasmine said excitedly.

But before Trixi could reply there was a shout behind them. "Coming through! Oh dearie me! Mind out! I think I'm going to crash!"

Let the Ceremony Begin!

"Whooooaaaaa!" King Merry yelled as
he flew through the trees towards them
on a very wide leaf. He was pixie-sized
too! His crown had fallen across one eye
and his white curly hair was standing up
on end as he swerved from side to side.

"Hello, my friends!" he cried, letting
go of his leaf for a moment to wave.

"Whoops!" he gasped again as the leaf spun round and he almost fell over the edge. "Swords and sceptres, flying a leaf is harder than it looks!" He grabbed the edges again. "Come on, leaf, that way! Take me over to my friends!"

The leaf lurched from side to side as it approached them, almost tipping King Merry into a huge blackberry bush.

"He's even more wobbly than Molly is on her bike!" Ellie grinned.

King Merry's leaf reached them and sank down to the ground. "Oh, that feels better," the king said, sighing with relief as he tottered off. "I'm not really sure I'm cut out for flying." He mopped his forehead with a large hanky embroidered with crowns.

"I think you were doing very well, Your

Majesty," said Trixi loyally.

King Merry smiled at her. "Thank you, Your Highness," he said, bowing down as low as far as his rather round tummy would allow.

Trixi blushed. "Oh, please don't bow to me, King Merry. It feels wrong."

"No, it doesn't, my dear," said King Merry. "You are now the pixie princess and it is right I should bow to you when we are in your realm – the Leafy Lands."

He smiled at Trixi and his eyes twinkled happily. "And the pixies couldn't wish for a better leader!"

"So who will be in charge of the Graduation Ceremony?" Jasmine asked.

"Why, Trixi, of course," said King Merry. "I only used to rule over it because there was no pixie princess."

Trixi looked anxious. "But I don't know what to do!"

"Don't worry, Trixi," the little king reassured her. "I'll be there beside you the whole time and tell you everything."

"Oh, thank you," Trixi breathed.

Just then there was a shout. "Trixi! There you are. Everyone's looking for you. The ceremony is about to start!"

It was Petal. She was wearing a pretty daffodil-yellow dress and a headband of woven wild flowers on her head. She flew up to Trixi and then stopped as if she was a bit unsure.

Trixi reached out and hugged her and Petal looked relieved. "I didn't know if I was still allowed to hug you anymore."

"Of course you are!" said Trixi. "Oh, I wish everyone would stop treating me differently. I feel just the same as ever!"

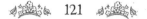

"You'll be fine, my dear," said King
Merry kindly. "Now, it sounds like we'd
better get a move on. Come on! Come
on!" He jumped back on to his leaf.
"Giddy-up leaf!"

The leaf lunged forwards into the air
and King Merry tumbled straight off the
back. Trixi quickly tapped her pixie ring
and a giant cushion appeared beneath
him. He bounced onto it. "Oh my
goodness gracious!" he said, blinking and

sitting up. "I really haven't got the hang of this leaf at all!"

"Why don't we all go on *my* leaf?" Trixi suggested hastily. With a secret smile at the girls she tapped her ring, making her leaf grow bigger. "It'll be much...er... quicker."

The girls helped King Merry up and they all climbed onto Trixi's leaf.

"Here we go!" said Trixi, making her leaf rise smoothly into the air.

As they got closer to the Heart Tree, they saw that all the other pixies were hovering around the trunk and sitting on the lower branches. In front of them, a small platform jutted out from the side of the tree. It was decorated with garlands of brightly-coloured flowers.

"We'll all sit on the stage," said Trixi. "I'd better find us some chairs." She tapped her ring.

"Princess magic bring us each a seat,
So we can sit and rest our feet."

Her ring and crown both glowed brightly and suddenly five seats appeared on the stage. There were two golden

thrones and three very comfy-looking armchairs, one with pink cushions, one with green and one with blue.

Summer, Ellie and Jasmine exchanged delighted smiles.

As Trixi's leaf flew onto the stage and landed the waiting pixies cheered and clapped.

"It's the pixie princess and King

Merry!" they called.

"And Summer, Ellie and Jasmine!"

"Hooray for Princess Trixibelle!" someone shouted.

"Three cheers for the king and his Very Important Friends!"

Trixi's cheeks flushed pink and she looked a bit embarrassed, but she waved at everyone and then sat down on her throne. King Merry and the girls took

their seats too. Summer saw Trixi's mum, Bluebell, waving at them and waved back. Suddenly Trixi tapped her pixie ring and the sound of trumpets filled the air.

Jasmine squeezed her friends' hands happily. This was so exciting! Graduation Day was about to begin!

A Horrible Shock

As the trumpets sounded, the pixies that were about to graduate formed a circle. Silence fell and everyone looked at Trixi expectantly. She gulped.

"Welcome, everyone!" Trixi's voice shook slightly and she broke off. She gave the girls a nervous look. "I can't do this," she whispered.

"Yes, you can. Remember how brave you were when you fought Queen Malice yesterday," whispered Jasmine.

"And how you sent her away from the woods," added Summer.

"And how the Heart Tree chose you to be the next princess," Ellie reminded her.

"You *can* do this, my dear," said King Merry. "I know you can."

Jasmine nodded. "You don't have to do anything special. Just pretend you're talking to us and be yourself."

Their words seemed to help. Trixi lifted her chin and her voice became stronger. "Welcome to our Graduation Ceremony! Today is a very special day for all pixies and I'm delighted that the king and his three Very Important Friends are able to be here with us. I would also like to welcome our other guests, our friends in the woods!" She swept her arms out.

To the girls' astonishment, the tall slender trees around the Heart Tree started to shimmer and the bluebirds in their branches fluttered up into the sky. One by one the trees sparkled and disappeared, leaving a slim figure standing where each tree had once been. The people had beautiful pale faces, long hair and were dressed in clothes of all different shades of green. They waved their hands and smiled at the pixies.

They were each about the size of a
normal human but to the pixie-sized girls
they looked incredibly tall.

"Who are they?" whispered Summer.

"Wood nymphs," King Merry
explained. "They share the Leafy Lands
with the pixies. They're gentle, kind
people who protect the woods and the
creatures who live in the trees."

"They always come and watch our
Graduation Ceremony," Trixi added as
the bluebirds flew down and perched on
the wood nymphs' shoulders.

Jasmine looked at the waiting pixies.
Petal was hopping from one foot to the
other in excitement. "I think Petal's going
to burst if the ceremony doesn't start
soon!" she laughed. "I wonder what sort
of leaf she'll get."

Trixi held up her hands for silence. "It is time for the ceremony to begin. Would the first graduate pixie step forward – Daisy Fairweather!"

A pixie with strawberry blonde hair and dancing brown eyes stepped up to the stage.

"So, Daisy, do you know what you would like your grown-up leaf to be like?" Trixi asked.

"I'd like it to be able to fly through water," said Daisy eagerly.

"Let's see what the
Heart Tree thinks," said
Trixi with a smile.

Daisy walked up to
the tree and pressed
both her hands to
the trunk. She called
out:

*"Somewhere on the
great Heart Tree,
A little leaf is meant for me!"*

There was a tinkling sound as the
leaves started to rustle. Suddenly one
leaf detached itself from the branches. It
twirled down towards them, changing
shape as it fell. But suddenly the pixies
started to shout out and point. The falling
leaf was turning darker and curling up at
the edges.

Ellie, Summer and Jasmine looked at each other in surprise. Was this supposed to happen?

The leaf began to shrivel up, getting darker and darker. By the time it landed on the ground it was completely black. The pixies were all talking and shouting at once. The girls didn't have a clue what was going on.

Daisy burst into tears and Petal and some of her other friends ran to comfort her.

King Merry shook his head. "Oh, goodness gracious me. This isn't good.

This isn't good at all," he said over the noise of the confused pixies.

"What's happening?" asked Ellie in confusion.

King Merry's kindly face looked worried. "The leaves don't normally look like that. Oh dearie me, I have a dreadful feeling that this has something to do with my horrible sister."

Summer swallowed. "With Queen Malice?"

A jeering cackle rang out through the clearing. "Did somebody say my name?"

The pixies shrieked and looked around. "It's Queen Malice! Queen Malice is here!"

"But Queen Malice can't be here," protested Jasmine. "Trixi's spell stopped her coming anywhere near the Heart Tree."

The laughter rang out again. "You fools! I don't have to be nearby to cause trouble for you all!"

"Sister? Where are you?" demanded King Merry.

Ellie suddenly realised the queen's voice was coming from near the floor. She looked down. "There!" she cried, pointing

at the leaf, her heart skipping a beat.
"Look, everyone!

Queen Malice's face was shimmering
in the blackened leaf. "So, you think
you can stop me, do you, you pointless
princess?" she jeered at Trixi. "Well,
think again! You might have kept me
from getting close to your precious tree,
but you didn't think to banish my Storm
Sprites too!"

There was a harsh
jeering and cackling
overhead and five
sprites zoomed up
out of the branches
at the top of the
tree. They swooped
down, pulling faces
at the pixies.

"You'll never stop Queen Malice!" they hooted. "She's got a plan to get your silly crown!"

The wicked queen shrieked with laughter. "You have done well, my Storm Sprites! From now on, any leaf that falls from this tree will wither and die. No more pixies will get their new leaves until you give me the pixie princess's crown!" Her laughter shrieked out, fading away as her image in the leaf disappeared.

There was uproar in the clearing. The bluebirds flew around in panicky circles and all of the pixies and wood nymphs were talking and shouting at once.

"What are we going to do?"

"No one will be able to graduate!"

Petal burst into tears. "No new pixies will get their leaves and fly."

Daisy was sobbing too. "We won't be able to be proper grown-up pixies with our own special jobs now."

Trixi turned to the girls and King Merry. "What should I do? This is awful! I have to give Queen Malice my crown."

"No!" Summer gasped. "You can't!"

"We'll work out what the Storm Sprites have done," Jasmine declared. "And find a way to stop them!"

"Let's search the tree," said Ellie.
"Maybe we'll find a clue."

"Ask everyone who can fly to help,
Trixi!" urged Summer.

Trixi raised her hands and the pixies
fell silent. All except one. High up in the
Heart Tree, one of the pixies cried out.
"Attack! Help! We're being attacked!"

The tree's branches had started to shake
violently.

"It's the Storm Sprites!"
realised Summer.

The Storm Sprites
were shaking the
branches, trying to
make the pixies fall
off!

"Help!" shrieked
Bluebell, hanging on for dear life.

Trixi gasped but before she could move, another pixie flew her leaf over and rescued Bluebell. Trixi breathed a sigh of relief.

King Merry shook his fist. "Stop it right now, you horrible mean things!

The sprites crowed with laughter. "Why would we listen to you, King Titchy!"

"We're not going to stop!" jeered another. "And you can't make us!"

"Silly pixies sitting in a tree! Shake

them off – one, two, three!" the sprites chanted, shaking the branches again.

The pixies grabbed their flying leaves and leaped on them before they fell.

"Come on," Trixi shouted to the girls. "I'm going to stop those Storm Sprites!" The girls jumped onto her leaf with her.

"Oh, do be careful," cried King Merry wringing his hands as Trixi's leaf shot upwards with the girls clinging on.

"What's your plan, Trixi?" asked Jasmine.

But before Trixi could answer, her leaf started to judder and shake.

"What's happening now?" gasped Ellie, feeling sick with fear.

"I don't know!" cried Trixi in alarm as the leaf lurched to one side. "It never usually behaves like this."

"It's not just this leaf!" cried Jasmine.

"Look! Everyone's in trouble!" All the leaves around them were starting to sway and tip.

"Whatever the Storm Sprites have done must be affecting the flying magic of *all* the leaves," said Summer.

"Can we go down now please?" Ellie stammered as the leaf lurched to one side. Then, suddenly, it seemed to lose all its flying power!

"I don't think we've got any choice!" cried Trixi as the leaf plummeted towards the ground...

Naomi's Plan

Ellie shut her eyes as they hurtled towards the forest floor.

"Aaaaagggghhh!" all three girls screeched as the ground got closer and closer. Just when they were sure they were about to crash, a pair of huge hands caught them and lifted them up safely.

They opened their eyes and looked into the face of a beautiful wood nymph with brown hair the colour of a ripe conker and hazel eyes.

"Are you all right?" the wood nymph said anxiously.

"Oh, yes," gasped Trixi. "Thank you so much for catching us, Naomi!"

Summer glanced around and saw to her relief that the other wood nymphs were catching the other falling pixies. Soon every pixie was safe.

"What's happening?" asked Naomi.

"It must be the Heart Tree," said Trixi.
"The tree gives the leaves their flying
power – and whatever the sprites have
done is taking it away!"

"We have to find out what's going on
and fix it." Jasmine said.

"I think I've got enough power to try
and make my leaf fly, but not all the
leaves," said Trixi. The pixie looked at
the Storm Sprites circling the tree and
her shoulders dropped. "But even if I *can*
make my leaf fly, we've still got to get
past the sprites."

"I could help you with them," said
Naomi.

"How?" said Ellie.

Naomi smiled mysteriously. "If you can
get them to fly towards me you'll see!"

She carefully placed the girls, Trixi and
the leaf back onto the graduation stage
and then stepped away
from the Heart Tree.
Suddenly her body
started to shimmer.
The girls gasped
as she turned
back into
a slender
tree, her body
becoming the
trunk and her
raised arms turning
into twiggy branches.

"I hope Naomi can
help," said Trixi. "We have
to stop the Storm Sprites.
Look at them!"

The sprites were still shaking the branches, laughing spitefully as the pixies tumbled out and the wood nymphs ran to catch them.

Trixi tapped her ring.

"Princess magic come to my aid,
My leaf must fly, its powers not fade."

Her crown flashed with light and suddenly the leaf glowed all over as if it was coated with millions of tiny emeralds. "Come on," Trixi cried. The girls leaped on. They flew up towards where the sprites were shaking the branches.

"Bet you can't catch us!" Trixi cried.

Jasmine blew a raspberry.

Ellie stuck her tongue out and pulled a face. "Yeah! You're too slow!"

The sprites stopped shaking the
branches and scowled. "We're not slow!"

"Oh, yes you are," shouted Jasmine.
"You're slower than snails."

"Oh really?" said a sprite.

"We'll see about that," snapped another
sprite. "After them!"

The sprites flapped into the air.

Trixi's leaf zoomed upwards like a rocket. The sprites flew underneath her and bashed into each other, bumping their heads together.

"OW!" they all shrieked.

Trixi turned a loop-the-loop. "Still think you can catch us?"

"YES!" screamed the sprites furiously, racing after her again. Trixi darted her leaf from side to side as fast as a swallow. Ellie shut her eyes tight and Summer put her arms around her. It was like being on a wild roller-coaster! Glancing behind, Summer could see the sprites catching up, their bony fingers reaching out...

Suddenly Trixi made the leaf drop down. She headed straight for Naomi's outstretched branches, with the sprites racing close behind them.

"What's Naomi going to do?" cried Jasmine, her hair flying back from her face as they clung on.

As they swooped out through the branches they found out. SNAP! Naomi's branches closed around the five sprites, imprisoning them in a twiggy cage.

"NO!" yelled the sprites, thumping at the branches and flapping their wings.

"Let us out!"

But the branches just tightened further around them. They were completely trapped!

"This is your fault!" one screamed at another.

"No, it's yours, bird brain!" he shouted back.

As the sprites squabbled and fought, the tree's branches shook gently as if Naomi was laughing.

"Thank you," Trixi beamed, flying up to the trunk. "Thank you so much!"

The tree bent gracefully towards them for a moment in a bow.

"Well, that's the sprites sorted out!" said Jasmine. "Now we just need to find out what Queen Malice got them to do to the Heart Tree. Come on!"

Trixi flew her shimmering leaf towards the tree. All the leaves on the lower branches looked as healthy and pretty as usual.

"Let's fly higher," said Summer.

They went up and up, swooping through the leaves and checking each branch, but they didn't find anything.

"The Storm Sprites must have done *something*," said Ellie in frustration.

"Wait!" said Jasmine, peering upwards towards the top branches. "What's that? Right at the top of the tree?"

They all shaded their eyes and looked towards the topmost branches. There was something large, black and spiky there.

Trixi flew closer. A horrible dark stain was spreading down the tree bark and now they could see where it was coming from. In the very top branches was one of Queen Malice's horrible thunderbolts!

Cracking a Thunderbolt

The girls stared at the thunderbolt. It was nestled in the tree like a big black monster, the darkness leaking down from it and spreading branch by branch through the tree.

"The Storm Sprites must have put it there," said Trixi in dismay. "If the darkness reaches the roots the Heart Tree will never recover!"

"What are we going to do?" said Summer.

But before Trixi could reply, the leaf beneath them started to shake and judder again. "Oh, no!" said Trixi, her face going pale. "The thunderbolt must be the thing that's blocking the flying magic in the leaves, and now we're so close to it, it's affecting us too! We've got to get away from here!"

She turned the leaf around and swooped away. As they got further from the thunderbolt, her leaf stopped shaking.

"That was close," said Trixi.

Ellie gulped. This adventure had far too much flying in it for her liking!

"We've got to get rid of that thunderbolt," said Jasmine.

"But how?" asked Summer. "It's much

too big for us and the other pixies to move, and we can't fly close enough to reach it anyway."

They all exchanged anxious glances. What could they possibly do?

Trixi looked close to tears. "Oh, this is awful. I'm the pixie princess! I'm supposed to be protecting the other pixies but I can't think of what to do. I'm a useless princess!"

Summer hugged her. "No, you're not."

"Not at all," said Ellie, hugging Trixi too. "The Heart Tree picked you because you're amazing, Trixi."

"It's going to be okay," said Jasmine, joining in the hug. "We just need to work together like we always do."

Trixi blinked back her tears. "Thank you."

"Why don't you take us back down to the graduation stage, Trixi?" suggested Jasmine. "We can tell everyone what we've discovered."

Trixi headed back down. The Storm Sprites were still caught in their twiggy cage, shouting and squabbling. The bluebirds had settled themselves on Naomi's branches and were twittering at the sprites teasingly. The pixies clustered around the stage as Trixi landed. All their

leaves were lying on the floor, looking
dull and lifeless.

"Did you find anything, Trixi?" cried
Petal.

"What's wrong with the tree?" Bluebell
asked.

King Merry came hurrying over.
"What has my dreadful sister done this
time?"

Trixi quickly explained what they had found out. There was a gasp of horror from the crowd as she told them about the thunderbolt and the darkness seeping from it.

"You can see it coming down the tree now!" cried Petal, pointing upwards. They all followed her gaze and saw that she was right. The darkness was creeping down the tree trunk, centimetre by centimetre, blackening and twisting the beautiful leaves.

"Oh, thrones and sceptres!" exclaimed King Merry. "We've got to get rid of that thunderbolt."

"But how?" Summer cried. "We can't fly up to it because it takes flying magic away."

"Maybe we could put ropes around it and pull it down," said Jasmine.

"But we can't get close enough to do that," pointed out Ellie. She frowned. "We've broken the spell on Queen Malice's thunderbolts before. What did we do then?"

"Well, when we were at Glitter Beach the thunderbolt took away all the sand…" Summer started.

"But we broke the spell and made the thunderbolt crack by putting some grains

of sand back on the beach," Jasmine remembered.

"And when we were at the Enchanted Palace we cracked the thunderbolt by putting on a show when Queen Malice tried to ruin it," Ellie added.

"It was a wonderful show!" King Merry nodded.

Ellie looked excited. "And it broke the spell! That's it – if we want to break the spell we have to do what this thunderbolt is trying to stop!"

"Queen Malice is trying to take away the pixies' flying power so we'll give up and give her the crown," said Summer.

"Which we'll never do!" Jasmine said firmly.

Ellie grinned. "Queen Malice wants to *stop* the pixies flying, so, maybe if we get everyone to fly then the spell will break?"

"I think you're right!" said Summer.

"It's very clever of you to work it out!" said King Merry, looking impressed.

"But how do we get everyone to fly?" said Trixi. "I haven't got enough magic to make all the leaves work again."

There was silence as they all thought

about it. Just then, a bluebird swooped overhead, giving Summer an idea. "I know! Why don't we fly on the back of the bluebirds?"

Trixi stared. "That's brilliant, Summer!"

"More flying," said Ellie with a gulp.

"Yes, but think how much fun it will be!" said Jasmine. Flying on the back of one of the pretty little birds with their soft blue feathers sounded amazing.

"I'm sure the birds will help," said King Merry. "Why don't you ask them, Trixi?"

Jasmine hugged Trixi. "We've beaten Queen Malice once already. Now it's our chance to beat her again."

Trixi lifted her chin. "You're right. We can do it – I know we can!"

Take That, Queen Malice!

Trixi tapped her pixie ring and her crown began to sparkle with light. She called out:

"Feathered friends, please hear my plea,
We want to save our dear Heart Tree.
We need to ride into the sky,
On your backs, flying high!"

"Oh, I hope it works," said Summer, gripping King Merry's hand.

"It *is* working – look!" the king cried, his glasses wobbling on his nose as he craned his neck to look up at the sky. "Here come the bluebirds!"

Bluebirds swooped down and landed beside the pixies. They were only small birds, but to the pixie-sized girls they were the size of horses!

They twittered happily at Trixi.

"Thank you for coming, friends. We really need your help!" Trixi said. "Please may we ride on your backs and fly into the sky?"

The birds flapped their wings and nodded their heads happily.

Trixi walked up to the nearest one and stroked his smooth feathers before scrambling up onto his back. Summer chose a very pretty bird with feathers as bright blue as a forget-me-not.

Ellie chose a sturdy, safe-looking bird and Jasmine chose one of the smallest who looked like he would be very fast!

"Come on, everyone – join us!" Trixi told the other pixies. "We need to get every single pixie into the air!"

The pixies ran forwards and started to get on to the birds' backs. Bluebell was one of the first, followed by Daisy Fairweather. Even Aunt Maybelle found an elegant-looking bluebird to fly on.

"NO!" shrieked the Storm Sprites from their twiggy cage. "You can't do this!"

"Oh, yes, we can!" cried Trixi. Her bird flew into the sky. The others all followed. "Come on, everyone! Let's fly as high as we can!"

They all flew up until they could see the menacing thunderbolt with its spiky sides.

"But we're all flying!" Ellie groaned. "Why hasn't it broken yet?"

Jasmine peered over her bluebird's wing. Far down on the graduation stage a tiny pixie was waving frantically. It was Petal!

"I'll get her!" Jasmine said, urging her bluebird into a daring dive.

"They went without me!" Petal sobbed as she got closer.

"Never mind," Jasmine comforted the little pixie. "We can share!" Her bluebird chirped in agreement. Jasmine slid over

and Petal climbed up behind her. The second the bluebird flapped back up into the air, there was a deafening CRACK! The thunderbolt had split in half!

"Hooray!" cheered Jasmine, zooming from side to side on her bird with Petal holding tight around her waist.

"It's broken!" cried Summer.

"And the spell's broken too!" said Ellie, pointing. The dark stain was vanishing from the tree trunk as if it had never been there.

The birds flew in a delighted circle, swooping and diving. The girls laughed out loud – even Ellie! On the ground below them every single flying leaf started to shimmer. One by one they rose into the air.

"Our leaves are back to normal!" cried

Bluebell.

"Hip hip hooray!" Petal cheered.

"Hip hip hooray for our pixie princess!" another pixie called.

"Hip hip hooray for King Merry!"

"Hip hip hooray for his Very Important Friends!"

Ellie, Summer and Jasmine felt as if
they would burst with happiness. Trixi
beckoned everyone down and the birds
carried them safely back to the stage.
The pixies slipped off the birds' backs
and conjured huge piles of seeds and nuts
for them to eat. The birds cheeped their
thank yous and tucked in happily.

"How will we find if the spell's really
gone?" asked Petal anxiously.

"Let's try the ceremony again!" said
Trixi. She clapped her hands. "Places
please!"

All the young pixies ran into their circle
again, and the other pixies jumped onto
their leaves and zoomed up to the lower
branches to watch.

"Petal, you come and try first!" called
Trixi.

Petal stepped forward, looking nervous.

"You know what you have to do," Trixi said gently.

Petal nodded and whispered.

"Somewhere on the great Heart Tree,
A little leaf is meant for me!"

There was a movement in the branches above and slowly one of the green heart-shaped leaves detached itself from its branch. It twirled all the way to the floor, changing shape and colour with every turn, becoming sleek and streamlined – a perfect leaf for flying up high. It landed on the ground and everyone breathed a sigh of relief. It was green and whole, not withered or black.

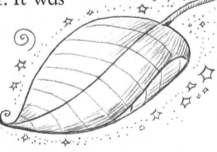

"The magic's working again!" said Trixi happily.

"And my leaf is exactly what I wanted!" Petal grinned.

Trixi smiled at the pixie, then cleared her throat. "It's a mountain pixie leaf," she said seriously. "I pronounce you a mountain pixie, Petal Greenwood." All the watching pixies cheered. Trixi's eyes shone. "Now everyone can graduate and get their grown-up leaf just as they should! Daisy, would you like to come forward again?"

"Trixi, what about the Storm Sprites?" Jasmine reminded her. She looked at the sprites sulking in their wooden cage.

"I'd better let them free," said Trixi. "We don't want them here spoiling our fun. Naomi!" she called. "Would you let the

Storm Sprites go, please!"

Naomi's tree shimmered. She threw
her branches up high,
tossing the sprites
away from the
clearing, then
turned back
to her wood
nymph form.
The sprites
flapped their
wings frantically to
stop themselves falling.

"Go now!" Trixi
commanded. "And never come here
again!"

"Or you might get stuck in another
twiggy cage!" Jasmine called with a grin.

The Storm Sprites shrieked angrily and

flew away shouting and arguing.

"Goodness, I'm glad they've gone," King Merry smiled. "They're horrible creatures. Now!" He rubbed his hands together. "Let's get on with this ceremony!"

Trixi nodded and beamed. "Daisy Fairweather, please step forward!" she called, and the Graduation Ceremony began.

One by one, the young pixies came up to the tree, said the magic words and received their leaves. They were all delighted with them.

"Now it's your turn!" Trixi said to the girls when all the pixies had got their leaves.

"Us? But we're not pixies," said Ellie in surprise.

"You're honorary pixies," declared
Trixi, "by Royal Decree of the pixie
princess. The Heart Tree would have been
destroyed without your help. You deserve
to have your own special leaves that will
appear whenever you turn into pixies in
the future!"

"Oh, wow!" breathed Jasmine in
delight.

Summer and Ellie grinned at one
another. There was nothing they wanted
more than to have their own pixie leaves.
What would they be like?

The three girls went up to the trunk
and said the words together. Three leaves
floated down. The one that landed by
Jasmine looked like it would go super-
fast and super-high. Summer's was a
very beautiful leaf that glimmered in all

different shades of green and Ellie's was a very wide leaf with curled up sides, a bit like the school leaves but extra-shiny.

"I love my leaf!" declared Jasmine. She was itching to try it out. "But what type of pixies are we, Trixi?"

Trixi smiled. "Jasmine Smith, Ellie Macdonald and Summer Hammond, I declare you all to be royal pixies because you're brave and adventurous and you help King Merry so much!"

The girls grinned in delight. Being royal pixies suited them just perfectly!

"I shall feel extra-safe flying on my very own leaf," Ellie said.

"When can we try them out?" asked Jasmine eagerly.

"Right now!" said Trixi.

Ellie, Summer and Jasmine hopped onto their leaves and soon they were zooming around the Heart Tree. All the other pixies joined in too, apart from Trixi.

She stood with King Merry, laughing and smiling and pointing out what different pixies were doing. They looked very happy and Summer felt glad that being the pixie princess wasn't going to stop Trixi from being King Merry's royal pixie too!

When everyone was tired from flying, Trixi used her magic to conjure up jugs of iced fruit punch and a massive cake. Each tier was in the shape of a heart and it had sugar leaves tumbling down the sides from the top to the bottom. It was the most delicious cake the girls had ever tasted. They sat on their leaves, hovering a few inches from the ground, munching happily.

Ellie licked the icing off her fingers. "I'm very glad we defeated Queen

Malice again."

"She'll never beat us!" declared Jasmine.

Summer smiled at Trixi who was conjuring up a large spotty napkin to tie around King Merry's neck, so he could eat the cake without getting his royal robes dirty. "I love being a pixie!"

"You'll have to come back and be pixies again very soon," said Trixi, overhearing. "But now I think it's time you went home."

"Only for a little while though," said King Merry, his eyes twinkling. "I'm sure my sister isn't going to be pleased that her plans to get the pixie princess crown have been stopped. She's bound to think of another wicked trick and then—"

"We'll be ready and waiting!" finished Jasmine. "Queen Malice can think up all the plans she likes but she isn't ever going to win!"

"Not ever!" Summer and Ellie agreed.

Trixi hugged them all and they hugged King Merry too.

"Goodbye!" they called, waving to all the pixies as Trixi tapped her ring.

"Goodbye!" the pixies shouted.

"Thank you for coming!" cried Bluebell and Petal.

"See you soon, dear friends," smiled

Aunt Maybelle.

A cloud of multicoloured sparkles surrounded the girls, whisking them away and setting them down gently.

"We're back!" Summer said, looking around. They were under the bush's thick branches, with the Magic Box between them.

"Another adventure over," Ellie sighed.

"Only until Queen Malice starts causing trouble again," said Jasmine.

"Or until King Merry and Trixi think of something fun for us to go to, like Graduation Day," said Summer.

"It feels like we've been away ages," Ellie said with a stretch.

"But to your mum and dad it'll be less than a minute," said Jasmine, putting the box back in her bag.

Summer stood up. "So who was *it* when we were playing tag?"

"You were!" Ellie and Jasmine shouted and with a squeal they dodged Summer's outstretched hands and leapt out of the bushes. Laughing and shouting the three best friends ran back down the pretty woodland path.

Join Ellie, Summer and Jasmine
for the next Secret Kingdom
adventure

Emerald Unicorn

Read on for a sneak peek...

A Disastrous Discovery!

"Snap!" cried Jasmine Smith. She picked up all the cards and beamed at her best friends Summer Hammond and Ellie Macdonald. "I win again!"

"Have you got cards hidden up your sleeves?" Ellie asked, giggling. "That's your third win in a row!"

Before Jasmine could reply, there was a

huge clap of thunder that rattled Ellie's
bedroom window. The girls jumped
up and ran to look out. The sky was
covered in thick grey clouds and rain was
pouring down. "Yuk!" sighed Summer.
"I don't think we're going to be able to
play in the garden at all today."

Lightning fizzed across the sky, then
more thunder boomed. Ellie shivered.
"Thunder always reminds me of Queen
Malice," she said. "I hate hearing thunder
when we're in the Secret Kingdom
because it means she's not far away."

"I wonder what she's up to right now,"
said Jasmine thoughtfully. "Something
horrible, I bet!"

The friends shivered at the thought.
They were the only people in the world
that knew about the Secret Kingdom,

a wonderful land filled with unicorns, mermaids, brownies and other magical creatures. It was ruled by kind King Merry, but his wicked sister, Queen Malice, was always trying to take over. With the help of their pixie friend, Trixi, the girls had defeated Malice lots of times before.

A tingle of excitement ran down Summer's spine as she thought about the Secret Kingdom. "We haven't been there for ages," she said. "I wish we could go back."

"It does seem a long time since we last heard from Trixi," Jasmine agreed. She took the Magic Box out of her bag and placed it on Ellie's bed. It was a beautifully carved box with a mirror in its lid, surrounded by six green gems.

The girls gathered round the box excitedly, then drew back with gasps of horror.

"What's wrong with it?" cried Ellie.

The carved pictures on the sides of the box had changed. Instead of beautiful unicorns, fairies and mermaids, there were Storm Sprites and huge mean-looking creatures! The green gems looked almost grey and the mirror was completely black. Peering into it was like looking into a bottomless black pool.

Summer shivered. "This isn't right," she said, gulping down a knot of fear that had risen in her throat. "The box has *never* looked like this before."

"It was okay when I checked it last week," said Jasmine with a frown. "Let's try to open it."

The girls put their hands on the gems on top of the box to see if it would magically open, but nothing happened. Then Jasmine ran her hands along the lid and pulled gently. But it was no good. The box stayed dark and firmly shut.

Summer took Ellie's and Jasmine's hands and squeezed them gently. "What if we can't go back to the Secret Kingdom ever again?" she asked in a shocked voice, saying aloud what they were all thinking.

"No, look!" cried Ellie. "Something's happening."

They all held their breath as a faint shimmer crossed the mirror for a moment, but it was nothing like the usual brightness that shone out when Trixi had a message for them. As the shimmer faded a picture started to appear!

"That's never happened before!" Ellie exclaimed. "What is it?"

Gradually the picture got clearer and clearer until the girls could see a familiar face in the blackened mirror. "King Merry!" Jasmine exclaimed.

"But what's happened to him?" Summer gasped.

The little king looked very unhappy and his white hair and beard hung in tangles. He wasn't wearing his crown and above his head was a barred window that let in just a little grey light.

"Is he in prison?" asked Summer, shocked.

"Girls," the king whispered anxiously. "I hope you get this message. The Secret Kingdom needs your help! I'm using the

Secret Spellbook to send you this, but I have to be quick. You MUST use one of your glitter dust wishes to call the Secret Spellbook to you. When it arrives, find a spell that will bring you to me."

The girls exchanged anxious looks. The Secret Spellbook contained old, powerful magic and was only ever used by the ruler of the Secret Kingdom. Things must be very bad indeed if King Merry wanted *them* to use the spellbook!

"Trixi can't come and get you this time," King Merry continued. "Keep watching and the Magic Box will show you everything. But you MUST call the spellbook to you as soon as you can. Oh dearie, dearie me!" Suddenly the picture of King Merry vanished and his wicked sister, Queen Malice, appeared in the mirror of the Magic Box.

As the girls watched, horrified, she picked up King Merry's crown from a golden table and placed it on her own head. "Now *I* rule the Secret Kingdom!" she cackled. She snatched up her thunderbolt staff and sent lightning streaking around the room.

"Isn't that King Merry's throne room?" asked Summer.

"I think so," agreed Ellie, aghast.

"Or it used to be," Jasmine said anxiously. As they watched, mud and slime began to ooze across the marble floor and the curtains changed from King Merry's royal purple to a horrid black. Cobwebs fell down from the ceiling and the cheerful portraits of King Merry changed into sneering pictures of the queen!

Queen Malice's Storm Sprites, nasty creatures with bat-like wings, came swooping down from the ceiling. They flew around the queen, cheering, as she stalked to King Merry's throne and sat down.

"What are *those* things?" asked Jasmine as several huge lumpy creatures lumbered into view. They had thick stumpy legs and long arms that reached to their knees. Their heads, which were the size of boulders, were dotted with clumps of bristly green hair. They bowed to the wicked queen. "Welcome, troll-friends," she said.

"Trolls!" Ellie whispered. "How could she let such horrible creatures into the palace?"

Suddenly, the picture faded and the

girls looked at one another in dismay. "She's done it at last," said Summer in a shocked voice. "Queen Malice is the ruler of the Secret Kingdom!"

Read

Emerald Unicorn

to find out what happens next!

Secret Kingdom

□ Got it   □ Got it

□ Got it   □ Got it

Series 5

Queen Malice has taken over the kingdom! It's up
to Ellie, Summer and Jasmine to find the jewels
King Merry needs to make a new crown –
or the horrid queen will rule forever!

Secret Kingdom

Sparkle Statue
☐ Got it

Melody Medal
☐ Got it

Pet Show Prize
☐ Got it

Twinkle Trophy
☐ Got it

ROSIE BANKS

Series 6

Queen Malice has stolen Ellie, Summer, Jasmine
and Trixi's special talents. Can they get them
back and save the kingdom?

Best Friends Day Quiz!

Fill in the answers to the quiz below to figure out which Secret Kingdom character you are most like. This will also tell you what kind of best friend you are!

Your best friend is upset, what do you do to cheer her up?
a) Tell her a joke
b) Offer to paint her nails
c) Ask her what is wrong and give her a cuddle

How would your best friends describe you?
a) Creative
b) Loud
c) Shy

How would you spend your perfect day with your best friends?
a) At home baking lots of yummy treats
b) At a dance class
c) At the zoo

You are planning a surprise for a new girl at school but you and your best friend have different ideas about what you should do. Do you…
a) ask someone else's opinion?
b) try to make them see that your idea is best?
c) let your best friend decide?

You see someone alone at playtime. What do you do?
a) Offer to plait her hair
b) Invite her to play with you
c) Offer her half of your snack to start the conversation

If you got mostly As you are most like Ellie!
You are funny and clever and artistic too! You like spending time at home and bring out the best in your friends. They love spending time with you!

If you got mostly Bs you are most like Jasmine!
You love fashion and are a very outgoing kind of friend to have. This means that you always have exciting ideas about what to do and you probably have lots of friends!

If you got mostly Cs you are most like Summer!
You are a very kind and thoughtful sort of friend. Always happy to go with the flow, you aren't the most forceful person but this means lots of people like to have you around!

Now you've worked out what kind of friend you are, don't forget that Best Friends Day is the 8th June 2014!
How about making your best friend a card or present? What else will you do to celebrate and show your best friend how special she is? Why not plan a day out together – a trip to the park, the playground or the cinema? Maybe you could bake some cupcakes to celebrate! Whatever you do – even if it's just a chat on the phone – make some time for your best friend, and have fun!